Arcee

Perceptor

Grimlock

Ironhide

Spike

When the Autobots were driven from their home planet of Cybertron by the Decepticons, they didn't give up hope. They established a new base on planet Earth, and instantly began to make plans to recapture Cybertron from their enemies.

Unknown to the Autobots however, there was a Decepticon spy in their midst: Laserbeak. When they were almost ready to move, he carried the news to Megatron, leader of the Decepticons, who wasted no time. The battle was on again – and this time there was yet another enemy against the Autobots. The giant metal planet, Unicron.

Designed by Howard Matthews
using colour photographs from the film.

British Library Cataloguing in Publication Data
Grant, John, 1930-
    Transformers – the movie.—(Transformers.
    Series 853; v. 7)
    I. Title   II. Series
    823'.914[J]   PZ7
    ISBN 0-7214-1009-X

First edition

Published by Ladybird Books Ltd Loughborough Leicestershire UK
Ladybird Books Inc Lewiston Maine 04240 USA

Printed in England

TRANS FORMERS THE MOVIE

story adaptation by John Grant

Ladybird Books

For many years, things had gone badly for the Autobots. They had fought hard against their enemies, the Decepticons. In the end, they had been driven from their home planet, Cybertron, but the Autobots never gave up hope. They made their base on planet Earth. They made friends with an Earth-boy, Spike. In the course of time, they were poised to recapture Cybertron. Two of Cybertron's moons were Autobot outposts. Moonbase 1 was military headquarters for the invasion, and Moonbase 2 was a forward observation post, manned by Bumblebee and... Spike, now a grown man.

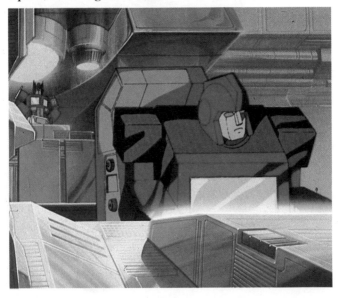

On Moonbase 1, Ironhide watched the monitor patiently, while the Autobot commander, Optimus Prime, studied the invasion plan. All the Autobots required now was a supply of energon cubes to power the invasion force.

Ironhide spoke. "I'm tired of this waiting, Prime. When are we going to start busting Decepticons?"

"Listen, Ironhide, we don't have enough energon cubes to power a full-scale assault," said Optimus Prime. "I want you to make a special run to Earth for another supply. Prepare the shuttle for launch."

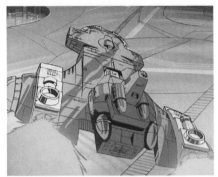

In a short time the shuttle was ready. Optimus Prime watched as it blasted off. "All we need," he said, "is a little energon...and a lot of luck!"

Just as he spoke, a cassette ejected from a console behind him. Unseen by Prime, it transformed into the Decepticon spy Laserbeak, who hurtled at top speed down to the surface of Cybertron to report to his leader, Megatron.

Megatron made his plans and issued his orders. The Decepticon spaceship lifted off from Cybertron, packed with Decepticons.

In the Autobot shuttle, Prowl and Ironhide sat at the controls. Cybertron was dropping behind fast when, without warning, a section of the shuttle wall exploded under a blast of laser fire. Decepticons poured in, and in moments the Autobot crew had been overcome.

Megatron was triumphant. "We will slip through Autobot security in their own shuttle! Autobot City will be destroyed! The Autobots will be vanquished for ever!"

On the other side of the galaxy, on planet Earth,
all was peaceful. Near Autobot City, a boy and an
Autobot were fishing. The boy was Daniel, the
young son of Spike, and the Autobot was his best
friend, Hot Rod. Daniel was looking glum. He
missed his father, far away on Moonbase 2.

"The shuttle from Cybertron is coming," he said.
"Let's watch it land."

Hot Rod transformed, and they sped to a look-out
point on a mountain high above Autobot City.

Daniel was watching the shuttle make its approach run through a telescope when he cried, "Hot Rod! Something's wrong! There's a hole in the shuttle!"

Hot Rod looked up. "Decepticons!" he cried.

In seconds the battle for Autobot City was raging. The city transformed to its fortress guise, and the defenders fought furiously against Megatron's army of Decepticon warriors. But they were outnumbered, and soon they were forced to fall back. Ultra Magnus, City Commander, sent a message to Optimus Prime to come to their help. Even as the message was going out, the Decepticons destroyed the Autobot communication centre.

Megatron prepared for the final attack as the mighty Devastator tore down the city defences. Then, with a roar of jets, Optimus Prime's relief force swept in over the battle. Autobots spilled from the shuttle, firing as they charged to the attack. The Decepticons found themselves caught in a deadly cross-fire: it was their turn to fall back.

Optimus Prime charged at the head of the warriors. Suddenly, in front, stood his arch-enemy ...Megatron!

"At last!" cried Optimus Prime. "One shall stand! One shall fall!"

Then, the two gigantic robots fell upon each other. Both were badly damaged by the time that Prime, with a last burst of strength, sent Megatron crashing from high on the city walls to the ground far below. There was a brief flicker of electricity, then the Decepticon leader lay still.

Starscream raced up with the remainder of the Decepticon force. "Astrotrain!" he cried. "Transform and get us out of here!" Soundwave picked up the battered Megatron and carried him aboard, then Astrotrain blasted off in a hail of Autobot fire, in full retreat back to Cybertron.

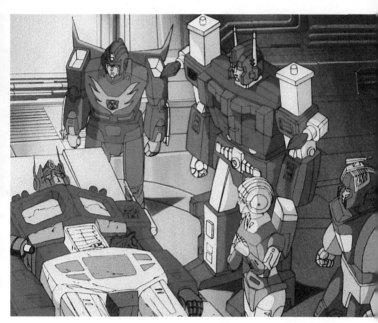

As the dust of battle settled, the Autobots
gathered about their fallen leader. His metal-work
was scorched and dented. Only a faint glow from

his eyes showed that he
was still functioning.
Optimus Prime was
dying.

In a faint voice, he said,
"Do not grieve. Ultra
Magnus, it is to you, old
friend, I shall pass the
matrix of leadership as it
was passed to me."

"I am not worthy of it,"
said Ultra Magnus. "I am
just a soldier."

"You will keep it," continued Optimus Prime, "until the day that an Autobot steps from your ranks and uses the power of the matrix to light our darkest hour." He opened the compartment in his chest and lifted out the crystal of pure energy. Then his strength failed and it dropped from his hand. Hot Rod caught it and passed it to Ultra Magnus. The new leader placed the glowing matrix in his own body cavity. As he looked down at Optimus Prime, his eyes began to shine with power. Optimus Prime's own eyes grew bright for a moment, then faded and went blank. He was dead.

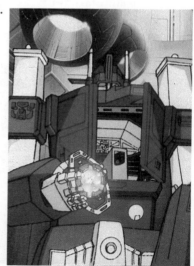

Out in the endless blackness of space, the passing of Optimus Prime flickered across a bank of monitor screens inside a strange, planet-like object. As big as a small world, the ringed and snow-capped metal sphere moved, not in a planetary orbit...but in a straight line towards Cybertron!

Aboard Astrotrain, the Decepticons were recovering from their defeat. The shuttle Decepticon laboured on full power. Starscream had taken charge, and Astrotrain spoke urgently to him. "If we don't jettison some weight, we'll never make it as far as Cybertron."

"You heard what he said?" said Starscream, looking round.

"It's the survival of the fittest," said Bonecrusher. Next moment a side-entry port was open, and the unhurt Decepticons began to throw the wounded out into space. Starscream dragged Megatron to the port and hurled him out after the rest. Lighter, Astrotrain blasted off, leaving the others adrift in space.

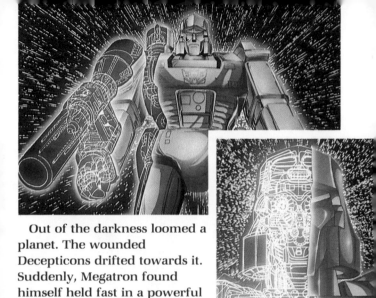

Out of the darkness loomed a planet. The wounded Decepticons drifted towards it. Suddenly, Megatron found himself held fast in a powerful magnetic beam. A deep voice spoke: "Welcome, Megatron! I am Unicron. I have summoned you here for a purpose. You are to destroy the Autobot matrix of leadership. I will provide you with a new body, and new warriors to command."

In a blaze of energy, Megatron was reconstructed as the mighty Galvatron. The broken remains of the

other Decepticons became aircraft-transformers under the leadership of Scourge and Cyclonus. Lastly, Unicron produced an immense new spaceship to lead Galvatron's armada.

"Now, go. Destroy the Autobot matrix!" roared the voice of the metal planet.

15

Meanwhile, Astrotrain had made it safely back to Cybertron. After a lot of argument, the Decepticons had accepted Starscream as leader. But now he wanted to make his leadership official. He summoned every Decepticon to the Hall of Heroes.

High above one end of the Hall stood the throne of the Decepticons. As the crowd of Decepticons looked on, Starscream stood in front of the throne, making a speech. On his head he wore a gold crown, and Thrust and Ramjet stood on either side of him. He paused for a moment. Like everyone else, he had heard the sound of distant jets. Then suddenly the Hall was filled as Galvatron and his warriors poured in.

"Who disrupts my coronation?" shouted Starscream.

"It is I, Galvatron," came the answer, as Galvatron transformed to his cannon shape and blasted Starscream out of existence.

As he transformed back, Starscream's crown rolled down the steps to the throne. Galvatron crushed it to fragments underfoot.

After only a little hesitation, the assembled Decepticons cried together: "LONG LIVE GALVATRON!"

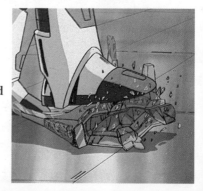

On Moonbase 1, Jazz and Cliffjumper looked out into space. Bearing down on them was a monstrous planet shape.

"Where'd that come from?" cried Jazz.

"Who cares?" shouted Cliffjumper. "I'm more worried where it's going!"

Quickly, Jazz called up Earth. "Talk to me, Earth! We got a situation out here!"

On Earth, repair work was going on at Autobot City. Blaster called, "I'm getting a faint signal!" He transformed, and the others listened to Jazz's voice. "...a weird-looking planet just showed up...and it's attacking Moonbase 1...!"

Back at Moonbase 1, Jazz
and Cliffjumper raced to
their shuttle and took off
as two giant claws gripped
Moonbase 1 and began to
drag it towards a vast
circular opening. As the
shuttle moved away,
Moonbase 1 was crushed
to fragments and sucked

inside. A moment later, with engines still at full
power, the shuttle was sucked in also.

Spike and Bumblebee watched in horror from
Moonbase 2. They had to do something. The base
contained a great store of explosives. Setting a
timer, they blasted clear in their shuttle. Once
more the claws gripped, and drew in Moonbase 2.
There came the roar of an explosion.

"It isn't even dented!" cried Spike. And next
moment they in turn were drawn into the interior
of the evil monster.

Daniel sat on Arcee's shoulder and watched helplessly as a video monitor showed the fate of Moonbase 2. "What about my dad?" he cried.

"Daniel, we'll do everything we can for Spike," said Ultra

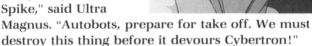

Magnus. "Autobots, prepare for take off. We must destroy this thing before it devours Cybertron!"

As they moved towards the shuttles, Springer pointed up and cried, "Look!" Diving to the attack were Galvatron and the Decepticons. At the same moment the Dinobots lumbered up to help their friends. In a hail of fire, the Autobots boarded the two space shuttles, followed by the Dinobots.

Soon they left the Decepticons far behind and the Autobots began to relax. In one shuttle, Kup put the controls on automatic while he told stories to Grimlock and the other Dinobots. Hot Rod put in some weapon practice with the auto-combatant.

The shuttles were cruising close past a large planet when the Decepticons struck again. The fight was fast and furious, and those in Ultra Magnus' ship saw the Dinobot shuttle suddenly spinning away trailing smoke and flames as it took a direct hit from a Decepticon missile.

The pursuing Decepticons swooped on the remaining shuttle. A cluster of missiles all struck at the same time, and the Autobot craft vanished in a blinding flash and a whirling cloud of fragments.

"The Autobots have been terminated!" cried Cyclonus.

As the Dinobots' shuttle disintegrated, Hot Rod was thrown clear. He found himself tumbling through space towards the planet he had seen seconds before the attack. He hit its surface just off the coast of a wide sea, and sank to the sea bed. Instantly he had to defend himself from a shoal of ferocious metallic fish. Fighting his way clear, he looked around him for a sign of the others. He saw nothing, but a sound came to him faintly through the water. It was Kup's voice, calling for help.

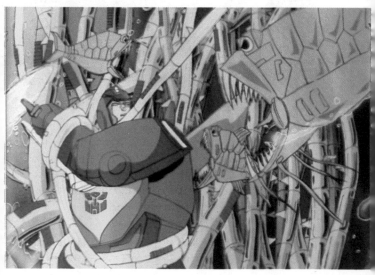

Hot Rod hurried in the direction of the sound, and found Kup...in the grip of a giant robot squid. The squid was pulling his victim apart.

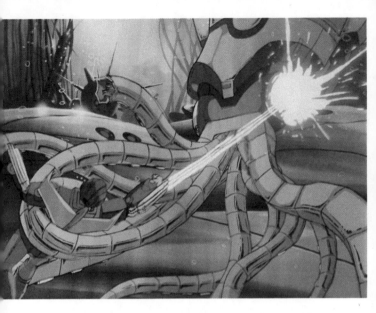

Hot Rod went to Kup's assistance. The squid gripped him in one of its tentacles, but a laser blast to the lens of one of its mechanical eyes sent it retreating in a cloud of black ink.

Hot Rod gathered up the scattered transformer pieces and carried them to the shore. There he reassembled his old friend, and Kup stood up and carefully tried all his moving parts. "You did an amazing job, lad. Amazing."

Then they transformed and set off to look for the Dinobots.

The two Autobots raced across the strange
planet. Suddenly they skidded to a halt, and
transformed back to robot shape. Their way was
barred by a band of ferocious-looking warriors.
Kup and Hot Rod walked forward.

Kup decided to try to make friends. "Don't act
hostile," he said to Hot Rod. "And don't make any
sudden moves."

But his efforts were in vain. The warriors suddenly transformed into evil, shark-jawed creatures. They piled on top of the Autobots, then dragged them

into a large complex where the two were locked in a barred cage. As the guards left, another prisoner looked through the bars of the adjoining cage.

"What is this place?" asked Hot Rod.

"This is Quintesson," was the reply. "It is the home of the Sharkticons who brought you here, and their masters the Quintessons. They hunt down the enemies of Unicron...a monstrous thing which devours other worlds. I am the only survivor of the destruction of my home planet."

"We've seen it," said Kup. "Now we know its name."

Suddenly, the Sharkticon guards appeared again. They seized the other prisoner and dragged him away. "I go to stand trial before the Quintesson ruler," he cried. "But, guilty or innocent, the sentence is always the same...death!"

Soon it was the turn of Kup and Hot Rod. Their arms were bound to their sides with energy bonds which also prevented them from transforming. Then they were led into the "court room".

A Quintesson with a rotating, many-faced head sat upon a high throne. The prosecutor stood below and waved long tentacles as Kup and Hot Rod were led onto a platform projecting high above a dark, water-filled pit.

The prosecutor addressed the figure on the throne. "Has Your Imperial Majesty reached a verdict? Guilty or innocent?"

"Innocent!" said the figure on the throne, and the platform dropped down, hurling Kup and Hot Rod towards the pit far below.

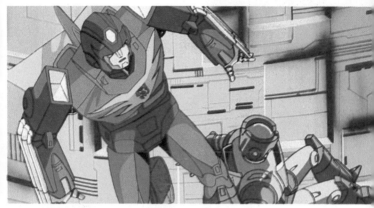

Just as the two Autobots hit the water at the
bottom of the pit, the energy bonds were released.
A second later they were attacked by a swarm of
Sharkticons. Kup and Hot Rod fought off the
monsters. But it was no use – still they kept coming.

"They've got more Sharkticons than we have
photon charges!" cried Hot Rod.

"Come on, let's hold a demolition derby," cried Kup, transforming. The Sharkticons were bowled over right and left as Kup and Hot Rod slammed into them. Then, racing around the sides of the pit at top speed, the two

Autobots shot to the surface and onto the floor of the trial chamber. The Sharkticons quickly followed, swarming out of the water. Although outnumbered, the Autobots still kept the Sharkticons at bay, piling them in heaps all around the sides of the pit and the walls of the chamber.

The Quintesson prosecutor raged as he saw the Sharkticons being destroyed by the two Autobot prisoners. He left his position below the throne and rushed to the side of the pool to take command. But before he could issue a single order, there was a thunderous crash. The great metal doors to the chamber toppled inwards. The prosecutor vanished underneath the doors. The next moment he was crushed completely

by the mighty weight of the Dinobots, Slag, Sludge and Grimlock as they trampled into the chamber and joined in the fight against the Sharkticons. Riding high on Grimlock's back was a small transformer.

Now, the Sharkticons were in retreat.

From the throne came a furious cry, "Sharkticons, execute them!"

Grimlock looked at the Sharkticons. "Me Grimlock say: execute *them!*" And he pointed to the rest of the Quintessons. It dawned on the Sharkticons that here was their chance to rid themselves of their Quintesson masters. Turning away from the Autobots, they swarmed across the chamber and up to the throne.

As the Quintessons fled before the Sharkticons, Kup said, "I think the problems on this planet will be solved very shortly."

"What about *our* problems?" asked Hot Rod. "We need a ship."

A cheery voice chanted, "You get a ship if I get a trip!"

"Who are you?" asked Hot Rod, in surprise.

"Him Wheelie. Him friend," said Grimlock. "Him help us find you."

"He'll be my friend, too, if he can find a ship," said Hot Rod.

Wheelie had already found one for them. Beyond the walls of the Quintesson complex rose the shape of the strangest ship the Autobots had ever seen.

Galvatron and his force sped through space to report to their master Unicron that Ultra Magnus and the matrix had been destroyed. Little did they know that the Autobots were safe, if a bit crowded, in the command pod of their shuttle. An emergency separation had allowed them to escape while the Decepticons blasted the empty shuttle with their missiles.

The pod however had not escaped without damage. "Perceptor, can you locate a place we can set down for repairs?" asked Ultra Magnus.

"There's the planet Junkion," replied Perceptor.

The battered shuttle swooped low over the junk-strewn surface of the planet and bounced and slithered to a halt. The Autobots started immediately on repairs. Daniel helped, clad in an exo-suit once worn by his father, Spike.

As they worked, they didn't see the Junkions observing them from among the heaps of junk. Suddenly, both Autobots and Junkions were startled by a roar of jets overhead.

"Decepticons!" cried Ultra Magnus. "We've got to draw them off and double back to the shuttle!"

But the first missiles blew the half-repaired ship to fragments. Trapped on the surface, the Autobots fought desperately as Decepticons came at them from all sides.

The Autobots made a fighting retreat down a long valley. The junk piled on either side gave some protection from the Decepticon fire. Ultra Magnus brought up the rear. He waited until the Autobots were clear, then he fired his laser weapon to bring down some of the junk as a barrier behind them. Now, he stood alone before the fury of the Decepticon attack. From a ridge nearby, Galvatron watched.

Ultra Magnus opened his chest compartment and took out the matrix. It pulsed with power, but a

special shield prevented its power from being released. Ultra Magnus pulled, but the shield remained firm.

"Prime!" he cried. "You said the matrix would light our darkest hour!"

Then, at a command from Galvatron, a flight of his evil warriors raced overhead, and a salvo of cannon fire blasted Ultra Magnus. Galvatron seized the matrix with a cry of triumph, and the battle was over. The Decepticons withdrew victoriously as quickly as they had arrived.

The Autobots looked in horror at the smoking remains of their leader. "First Optimus Prime. Now Ultra Magnus. And the matrix is gone," said Arcee. "What do we do?"

Before any of them could speak, there was a roar of motor cycle engines. The Autobots turned to see

the Junkions racing to give battle among the rusting piles of junk. And once again there came the sound of jet engines. Cruising over them was a weird spaceship. Familiar faces peered through the ports: Kup and Hot Rod, with the Dinobots, had arrived in the nick of time.

As the Autobots disembarked, the Junkions watched suspiciously. But Hot Rod and Kup persuaded them that the Autobots meant no harm, and finally made friends with them.

After a while, Wreck-Gar the Junkion leader announced that not only would they repair Ultra Magnus, but that they would join forces with the Autobots in pursuing Galvatron, winning back the matrix, and destroying Unicron.

Galvatron stood on Unicron, the matrix secured about his neck by a chain.

"Listen to me, Unicron," he said. "*I* now possess that which you wanted destroyed."

"Don't underestimate me, Galvatron," came the voice from deep within the evil planet. Next moment Galvatron fell to his knees as the surface upon which he stood began to shake. Unicron was moving forward towards Cybertron, and he was transforming… into a gigantic, horned, winged demon. Reaching

out, he began to tear at Cybertron with cruel, clawed hands. On the planet, the Decepticons scrambled to defend themselves. Galvatron transformed to his cannon shape and fired at Unicron. The monster picked Galvatron up between finger and thumb and swallowed him.

As Decepticons swarmed around Unicron, the Autobots and Junkions dived to the attack. One giant hand crushed the Junkion ship to fragments. A blast of fire blew a large piece out of the Quintesson craft and it crashed, out of control, through Unicron's eye and into the great, mechanical head.

Inside Unicron, the shattered Quintesson ship fell apart as it tumbled into the depths of the monster. The passengers were thrown out and landed in a heap...all except Hot Rod. "Where is he?" asked Daniel.

"I hope *they* didn't get him!" cried Springer, as down from the roof there sprang long cables armed with snapping metal jaws. They writhed and grasped at Daniel and the Autobots. Darting and dodging, the Autobots ran clear, but Daniel stumbled and fell. In an instant he was being attacked from all sides. Arcee

turned and fired several rapid shots, and the cables were severed, but a stray shot smashed an overhead pipe. A roaring torrent of liquid swept Daniel off his feet and down a long passage.

Struggling, Daniel was borne along by the liquid deep into Unicron. At last he fought clear and found himself looking up at a conveyor belt high above his head. Captured Decepticons were hanging from the conveyor and being dropped one by one into a cauldron of boiling acid. He heard a shout. It was his father and the Autobots from the Cybertron Moonbases. In a few more seconds they too would drop into the seething acid and be destroyed. Daniel was desperate.

He could see no way to stop the conveyor. Aiming the built-in weaponry of his exo-suit, he pressed the firing button. At the very moment that Spike and the Autobots dropped from the conveyor,

Daniel's shots shattered a hydraulic support, and a metal cover slammed down over the fuming cauldron.

"I did it!" cried Daniel, as he saw his father and the others land safely on the cover.

Out in space, the remaining Decepticons continued to attack Unicron. The Dinobots had regrouped and battered at the monster to get inside and rescue their friends.

Deep inside Unicron, Hot Rod slowly got to his feet. He had fallen much farther than any of the others. He was in a wide chamber littered with twisted metal and broken machinery. A dazzling light appeared, hanging in the shadows...the matrix!

Hot Rod took a step forward, and saw that Galvatron had the matrix.

"It will do you no good, Autobot!" cried Galvatron. "It cannot be opened!"

"Not by a Decepticon," replied Hot Rod.

The voice of Unicron echoed in the darkness, "Destroy him...or feel yourself torn limb from limb!"

Galvatron aimed a shot at Hot Rod, who transformed and raced away. Then he hurtled back to the attack. To and fro the fight raged. Then, Galvatron leapt on Hot Rod as he transformed back into his robot shape. The Decepticon leader seized his enemy around the neck and squeezed. "First Prime. Then Ultra Magnus," he snarled. "And now you. It's a pity you Autobots die so easily or I might have a sense of satisfaction now!"

Hot Rod's strength was ebbing rapidly as he looked up into the evil face of Galvatron. The matrix hung on its chain, and as Hot Rod looked into the pulsing crystal he heard in his mind the voice of Optimus Prime.

"Arise, Rodimus Prime!"

The matrix glowed ever brighter within its shield. Power surged through the body of the fallen Hot Rod. With a mighty heave he hurled Galvatron from him. Galvatron fired a shot, but it was deflected harmlessly by the matrix. Hot Rod picked up Galvatron. For a moment he held him above his head. "This is the end of the road, Galvatron!" he cried, and smashed the Decepticon through Unicron's metal side to be lost in the vastness of space.

Now, he picked up the matrix. The shield came off easily in his hands. Unicron screamed as the power of the matrix surged into him, then he pulled himself apart as he tried to stop the terrible thing which was destroying every corner of his body.

Daniel and Spike and the Autobots struggled
through the collapsing wreck that had been
Unicron. Suddenly, a tall and powerful Autobot
stood before them. Their new leader, Rodimus
Prime.

He cried, "Autobots...transform and roll out!"
"I knew you had potential, lad!" cried Kup.

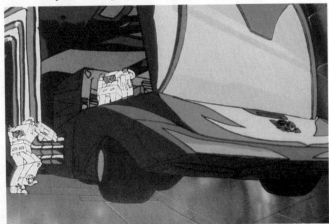

In a moment, the fleet of Autobot vehicles with Spike and Daniel aboard were racing for safety. With a splintering crash they burst through Unicron's remaining eye.

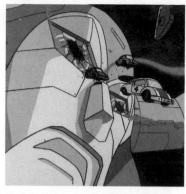

From Cybertron, the Autobots watched the evil Unicron explode into a million fragments. All that remained was the horned head orbiting the planet like a strange moon.

The struggle was over. Under the leadership of Rodimus Prime, the Autobots could begin to rebuild their home.

EVIL DECEPTICON

A Sharkticon

Starscream

Unicron

Laserbeak